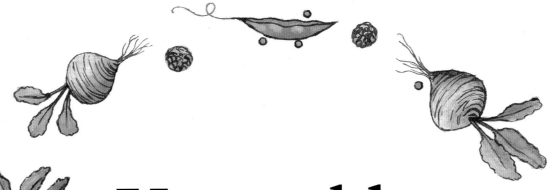

Vegetable
Glue

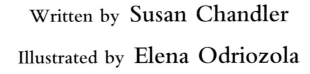

Written by **Susan Chandler**

Illustrated by **Elena Odriozola**

HUTTON
05039056

W hen my right arm fell off,
I knew what to do,

I stuck it back on,
With vegetable glue.

When my head rolled away,
I thought it had gone,

But I found it again,
And stuck it back on.

You can see for yourself,
That something's not right,
People don't fall apart.
It's just not polite.

I have to keep with me,
A big tub of glue,
To stick bits back on,
To make good as new.

Vegetable Glue

I hear you all shout,
'We've heard quite enough!
Tell us, how do we make,
That gloopy green stuff?'

'If our noses fall off,
Then what would we do?
Where would we buy
Some vegetable glue?'

Well, it's not in the shops,
And it's not on the telly,
Because vegetable glue
Is in everyone's belly.

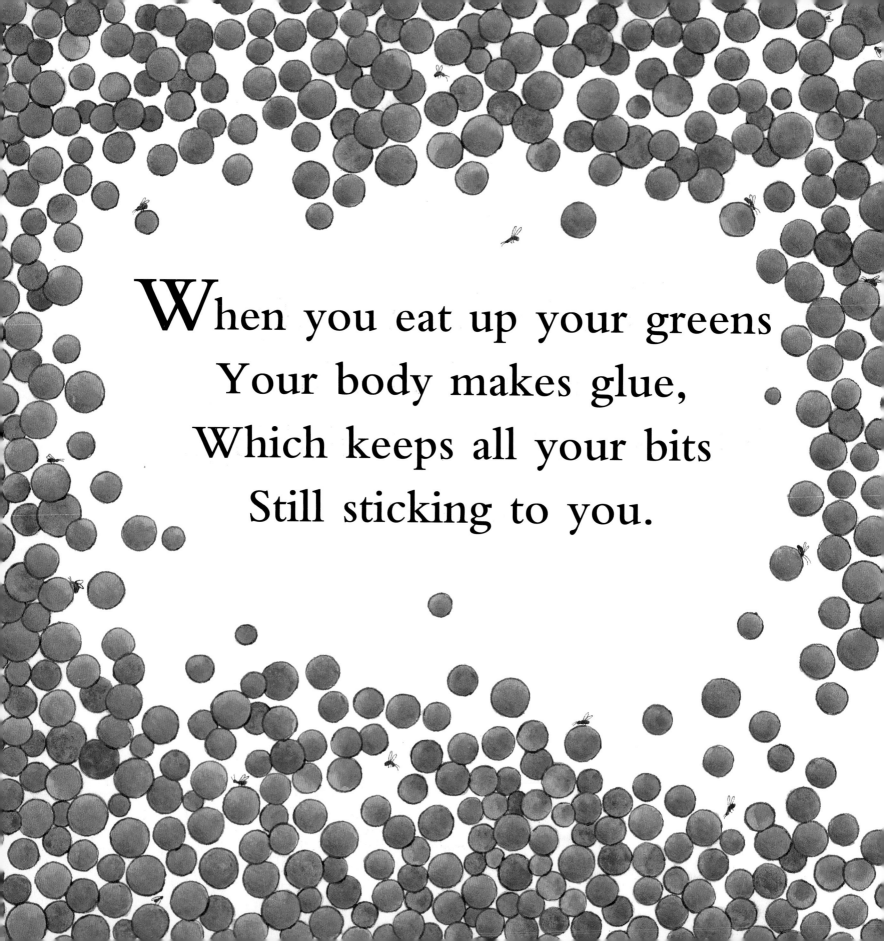

When you eat up your greens
Your body makes glue,
Which keeps all your bits
Still sticking to you.

But I was quite silly,
I made a mistake.
I wouldn't eat good things,
I only ate...

...cake!

I wouldn't eat cabbage,
Or turnips or beans,
I didn't like carrots,
I didn't like greens.

I didn't eat sprouts,
Now I've no special glue
No goodness inside me,
Like other kids do.

While others are playing,
I can't even cough.
If I sneeze or I burp,
Then something falls off.

Oops, pardon me
I've made a rude sound.
My bottom's dropped off

And is now...

... on the ground.

Now here is my granny
To give me some more.
She's looking quite good
For a hundred and four.

She'd like you to know
Why she's so fit and able.
She ate all her greens
Before leaving the table.

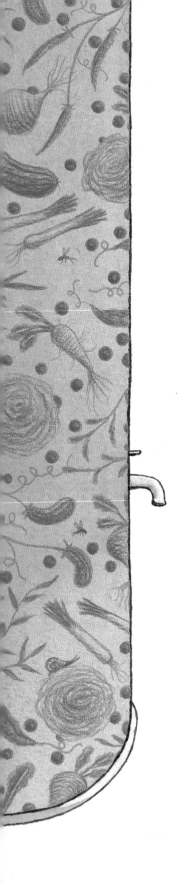

She ate all her greens
And I hope you do too,

Then...

you'll never need...

...Any vegetable glue.

For Chris and Ted

S.C.

For My Mothers

E.O.

Vegetable Glue

Text Copyright | Susan Chandler • Illustration Copyright | Elena Odriozola

The rights of Susan Chandler and Elena Odriozola to be have been asserted by them
in accordance with the Copyright, Designs and Patents Act, 1988

Published by Hutton Grove, an imprint of Bravo Ltd., in 2015
Sales and Enquiries:
Kuperard Publishers & Distributors
59 Hutton Grove, London, N12 8DS, United Kingdom
Tel: +44 (0)208 446 2440
Fax: +44 (0)208 446 2441
sales@kuperard.co.uk
www.kuperard.co.uk

Published by arrangement with Albury Books,
Albury Court, Albury, Oxfordshire, OX9 2LP.

ISBN 978-1-857338-15-7 (paperback)

A CIP catalogue record for this book is available from the British Library
10 9 8 7 6 5 4 3
Printed in China